Sunday Costs Five Pesos

A One-Act Comedy of Mexican Village Life

by Josephina Niggli

A SAMUEL FRENCH ACTING EDITION

SAMUEL FRENCH

FOUNDED 1830

New York Hollywood London Toronto

SAMUELFRENCH.COM

ISBN   978-0-573-62503-9   Printed   in   U.S.A.   #1010

MUSIC USE NOTE

Licensees are solely responsible for obtaining formal written permission from copyright owners to use copyrighted music in the performance of this play and are strongly cautioned to do so. If no such permission is obtained by the licensee, then the licensee must use only original music that the licensee owns and controls. Licensees are solely responsible and liable for all music clearances and shall indemnify the copyright owners of the play and their licensing agent, Samuel French, Inc., against any costs, expenses, losses and liabilities arising from the use of music by licensees.

IMPORTANT BILLING AND CREDIT
REQUIREMENTS

All producers of *SUNDAY COSTS FIVE PESOS* must give credit to the Author of the Play in all programs distributed in connection with performances of the Play, and in all instances in which the title of the Play appears for the purposes of advertising, publicizing or otherwise exploiting the Play and/or a production. The name of the Author *must* appear on a separate line on which no other name appears, immediately following the title and *must* appear in size of type not less than fifty percent of the size of the title type.

SUNDAY COSTS FIVE PESOS

THE CHARACTERS

As originally produced by the Carolina Playmakers at Chapel Hill, North Carolina, on April 25, 1936.

FIDEL, *who is in love with Berta*.....*Ralph Eichhorn*
BERTA .... *Ellen Deppe*
SALOME⎱ *friends of Berta....* ⎰ *Jessie Langdale*
TONIA ⎰ ⎱ *Christine Maynard*
CELESTINA .... *Jean Ashe*

THE SCENE: *A housed-in square in the town of the Four Cornstalks (Las Cuatro Milpas) in Northern Mexico.*

THE TIME: *The preesnt. Early one Sunday afternoon.*

5

Sunday Costs Five Pesos

THE SCENE: *A housed-in square in the town called the Four Cornstalks in the northern part of Mexico. On the Left of the square is the house of* TONIA *with a door and a stoop. At the back is a wall cut neatly in half. Left Center at back is the house of* BERTA, *and boasts not only a door but a barred window. On the Right Center at back is a square arch from which dangles an iron lantern. This is the only exit to the rest of the town, for on the Right side proper is the house of* SALOME. TONIA'S *house is pink, and* SALOME'S *is blue, while* BERTA'S *is content with being a sort of disappointed yellow. All three houses get their water from the well that is down Left Center.*

It is early afternoon on Sunday, and all sensible people are sleeping, but through the arch comes FIDEL DURAN. *His straw hat in his hand, his hair plastered to his head with water, he thinks he is a very handsome sight indeed as he pauses, takes a small mirror from his pocket, fixes his neck bandanna—a beautiful purple one with orange spots —and shyly knocks, then turns around with a broad grin on his face.*

BERTA *opens her door.* BERTA *is very pretty, but unfortunately she has a very high temper, possibly the result of her red hair. She wears a neat cotton dress and tennis shoes, blue ones. Her hands fastened on her hips, she stands and glares at* FIDEL.

7

BERTA. Oh, so it is you!

FIDEL. *(Beaming on her)* A good afternoon to you, Berta.

BERTA. *(Sniffing)* A good afternoon indeed, and I bothered by fools at this hour of the day.

FIDEL. *(In amazement)* Why, Berta, are you angry with me?

BERTA. *(Questioning Heaven)* He asks me if I am angry with him. Saints in Heaven, has he no memory?

FIDEL. *(Puzzled)* What have I done, Berta?

BERTA. *(Sarcastically)* Nothing, Fidel, nothing. That is the trouble. But if you come to this house again I will show you the palm of my hand, as I'm showing it to you now. *(She slaps him, steps back inside the door, and slams it shut.)*

FIDEL. *(Pounding on the door)* Open the door, Berta. Open the door! I must speak to you!

(The door of SALOME'S house opens, and SALOME herself comes out with a small pitcher and begins drawing water from the well. She is twenty-eight, and so many years of hunting a husband have left her with an acid tongue.)

SALOME. And this is supposed to be a quiet street.

FIDEL. *(Who dislikes her)* You tend to your affairs, Salome, and I will tend to mine. *(He starts pounding again. He bleats like a young goat hunting for its mother)* Berta, Berta.

BERTA. *(Opens the door again)* I will not have such noises. Do you not realize that this is Sunday afternoon? Have you no thoughts for decent people who are trying to sleep?

FIDEL. Have you no thoughts for me?

BERTA. More than one. And none of them nice.

SALOME. I would call this a lovers' quarrel.

BERTA. Would you indeed! *(Glares at FIDEL)* I would call it the impertinence of a wicked man!

FIDEL. *(Helplessly)* But what have I done?

SALOME. She loved him yesterday, and she will love him tomorrow.

8

BERTA. *(Runs down to* SALOME*)* If I love him to-morrow, may I lose the use of my tongue, yes, and my eyes and ears, too.

FIDEL. *(Swinging* BERTA *to one side)* Is it fair, I ask you, for a woman to smile at a man one day, and slap his face the next? Is this the manner in which a promised bride should treat her future husband?

SALOME. *(Grins and winks at him)* You could find yourself another bride.

BERTA. *(Angrily)* We do not need your advice, Salome Molina. You and your long nose—sticking it in everyone's business.

SALOME. *(Her eyes flashing)* Is this an insult to me? To me?

BERTA. And who are you to be above insults?

SALOME. I will not stay and listen to such words!

BERTA. Did I ask you to leave the safety of your house?

SALOME. *(To* FIDEL*)* She has not even common politeness. I am going! *(Crosses Right.)*

BERTA. We shall adore your absence.

SALOME. If this were not Sunday, I would slap your face for you.

BERTA. *(Taunting)* The great Salome Molina, afraid of a Sunday fine.

FIDEL. *(Wanting to be helpful)* You can fight each other tomorrow. There is no fine for week days.

SALOME. You stay out of this argument, Fidel Duran.

FIDEL. If you do not leave us I will never find out why Berta is angry with me. *(Jumps toward her)* Go away!

SALOME. *(Jumps back, then tosses her head)* Very well. But the day will come when you will be glad of my company. *(She goes indignantly into her house.)*

FIDEL. *(Turns to* BERTA*)* Now, Berta.

BERTA. *(Interrupting)* As for you, my fine rooster, go and play the bear to Celestina Garcia. She will appreciate you more than I.

FIDEL. *(With a guilty hand to his mouth)* So that is what it is.

BERTA. *(On the stoop of her own house)* That is all of it, and enough it is. Two times you walked around the plaza with the Celestina last night, and I sitting there on a bench having to watch you. *(Goes into the house.)*

FIDEL. *(Speaking through the open door)* But it was a matter of business.

BERTA. *(Enters with a broom and begins to sweep off the stoop)* Hah! Give me no such phrases. And all of my friends thinking, "Poor Berta, with such a sweetheart." Do you think I have no pride?

FIDEL. But it is that you do not understand—

BERTA. I understand enough to know that all is over between us.

FIDEL. Berta, do not say that. I love you.

BERTA. So you say. And yet you roll the eye at any passing chicken.

FIDEL. Celestina is the daughter of Don Nimfo Garcia.

BERTA. She can be the daughter of the president for all of me. When you marry her she will bring you a fine dowry, and there will be no more need of Fidel Duran trying to carve wooden doors.

FIDEL. *(His pride wounded)* Trying? But I have carved them. Did I not do a new pair for the saloon?

BERTA. Aye, little doors—doors that amount to no more than that— *(She snaps her fingers)* Not for you the great doors of a church.

FIDEL. Why else do you think I was speaking with the Celestina?

BERTA. *(Stops sweeping)* What new manner of excuse is this?

FIDEL. That is why I came to speak with you. Sit down here on the step with me for a moment.

BERTA. *(Scandalized)* And have Salome and Tonia say that I am a wicked, improper girl?

FIDEL. *(Measuring a tiny space between his fingers)* Just for one little moment. They will see nothing.

BERTA. *(Sitting down)* Let the words tumble out of your mouth, one, two, three.

FIDEL. Perhaps you do not know that the town of

10

Topo Grande, not thirty kilometers from here, is building a new church.

BERTA. *(Sniffs)* All the world knows that.

FIDEL. But did you know that Don Nimfo is secretly giving the money for the building of that church?

BERTA. Why?

FIDEL. He offered the money to the Blessed Virgin of Topo Grande if his rooster won in the cock-fight. It did win, so now he is building the church.

BERTA. *(Not yet convinced)* How did you find out about this? Or has Don Nimfo suddenly looked upon you as a son, and revealed all his secrets to you?

FIDEL. Last night on the plaza the Celestina happened to mention it. With a bit of flattery I soon gained the whole story from her.

BERTA. So that is what you were talking about as you walked around the plaza? *(Stands)* It must have taken a great deal of flattery to gain so much knowledge from her.

FIDEL. *(Stands)* Do you not realize what it means? They will need someone to carve the new doors. *(He strikes a pleased attitude, expecting her to say, "But how wonderful, Fidel.")*

BERTA. *(Knowing very well what* FIDEL *expects, promptly turns away from him, her hand hiding a smile, as she says with innocent curiosity)* I wonder whom Don Nimfo will get? *(With the delight of discovery)* Perhaps the Brothers Ochoa from Monterrey.

FIDEL. *(Crestfallen)* He might choose me.

BERTA. You? Hah!

FIDEL. And why not? Am I not the best wood carver in the valley?

BERTA. So you say.

FIDEL. It would take three years to carve those doors, and he would pay me every week. There would be enough to buy you a trousseau and enough left over for a house.

BERTA. Did you tell all that to the Celestina?

FIDEL. Of course not! Does a girl help a man buy a trousseau for another girl? That was why it had to appear as though I were rolling the eye at her. *(He is very much pleased with his brilliance.)*

BERTA. Your success was more than perfect. Today all the world knows that the Celestina has won Berta's man.

FIDEL. But all the world does not know that Fidel Duran, who is I, myself, will carve those doors so as to buy a trousseau and house for Berta, my queen.

BERTA. Precisely. All the world does not know this great thing— *(Flaring out at him)* And neither do I!

FIDEL. Do you doubt me, pearl of my life?

BERTA. Does the rabbit doubt the snake? Does the tree doubt the lightning? Do I doubt that you are a teller of tremendous lies? Speak not to me of cleverness. I know what my own eyes see, and I saw you flirting with the Celestina. Last night I saw you—and so did all the world!

FIDEL. *(Beginning to grow angry)* So that is how you trust me, your intended husband.

BERTA. I would rather trust a hungry fox.

FIDEL. Let me speak plainly, my little dove. Because we are to be married is no reason for me to enter a monastery.

BERTA. And who says that we are to be married?

FIDEL. *(Taken aback)* Why—I said it.

BERTA. Am I a dog to your heel that I must obey your every wish?

FLDEI. *(Firmly)* You are my future wife.

BERTA. *(Laughs loudly)* Am I indeed?

FIDEL. Your mother has consented, and my father has spoken. The banns have been read in the church! *(Folds his arms with satisfaction.)*

BERTA. *(Screaming)* Better to die without children than to be married to such as you.

FIDEL. *(Screaming above her)* We shall be married within the month.

BERTA. May this hand rot on my arm if I ever sign the marriage contract.

FIDEL. Are you saying that you will not marry me?

BERTA. With all my mouth I am saying it, and a good day to you. *(Steps inside the house and slams*

*the door. Immediately opens it and sticks her head
out)* Tell that good news to that four-nosed shrew of
a Celestina. *(Slams the door again.)*

*(FIDEL puts on his hat and starts toward the archway,
then runs down and pounds on TONIA's door, then
runs across and pounds on SALOME's. In a moment both girls come out. TONIA is younger and
smaller in size than either SALOME or BERTA and
has a distressing habit of whining.)*

SALOME. What is the meaning of this noise?
TONIA. Is something wrong?
FIDEL. I call you both to witness what I say. May I
drop dead if I am ever seen in this street again! *(He
settles his hat more firmly on his head, and with as
much dignity as he can muster, he strides out through
the arch.)*

*(The GIRLS stare after him, then at BERTA's door, then
at each other. BOTH shrug, then with one accord
they run up and begin knocking on BERTA's
door.)*

SALOME. Berta!
TONIA. Berta, come out!

*(BERTA enters. She is obviously trying to keep from
crying.)*

SALOME. Has that fool of a sweetheart of yours lost
his mind?
TONIA. What happened?
BERTA. *(Crying in earnest)* This day is blacker than
a crow's wing. Oh, Salome! *(She flings both arms
about the girl's neck and begins to wail loudly.)*

*(TONIA and SALOME stare at each other, and then
TONIA pats BERTA on the shoulder.)*

TONIA. Did you quarrel with Fidel?

13

SALOME. Of course she quarrelled with him. Any fool could see that.

BERTA. He will never come back to me. Never!

TONIA. *(To SALOME)* Did she say anything about the Celestina to him?

SALOME. *(To BERTA)* You should have kept your mouth shut on the outside of your teeth.

BERTA. A girl has her pride, and no Celestina is going to take any man of mine.

TONIA. But did she take him?

BERTA. *(Angrily to TONIA)* You take your face away from here!

SALOME. The only thing you can do now is to ask him to come back to you.

TONIA. *(Starting toward the archway)* I will go and get him.

BERTA. *(Clutches at her)* I will wither on my legs before I ask him to come back. He would never let me forget that I had to beg him to marry me. *(Wails again)* And now he will marry the Celestina.

TONIA. *(Begins to cry with her)* There are other men.

BERTA. My heart is with Fidel. My life is ruined.

SALOME. *(Thoughtfully)* If we could bring him back without his knowing Berta had sent for him— *(She sits on the edge of the well.)*

TONIA. Miracles only happen in the church.

SALOME. *(Catches her knee and begins to rock back and forth)* What could we tell him? What could we tell him?

TONIA. You be careful, Salome, or you will fall in the well. Then we will all have to go into mourning, and Berta cannot get married at all if she is in mourning.

SALOME. *(Snaps her fingers)* You could fall down the well, Berta! That would bring him back.

BERTA. *(Firmly)* I will not fall down the well and drown for any man, not even Fidel.

TONIA. What good would bringing him back do if Berta were dead?

SALOME. Now that is a difficulty. *(Begins to pace up*

and down at Left) If you are dead, you cannot marry Fidel. If you are not dead, he will not come back. The only thing left for you is to die an old maid.

Tonia. That would be terrible.

Berta. *(Wailing)* My life is ruined. Completely ruined.

Salome. *(With sudden determination)* Why? Why should it be?

Tonia. *(With awe)* Salome has had a thought.

Berta. You do not know what a terrible thing it is to lose the man you love.

Salome. I am fixing up your life, not mine. Suppose —suppose you did fall in the well.

Berta. I tell you I will not do it.

Salome. Not really, but suppose he thought you did. What then?

Berta. You mean—pretend? But that is a sin! The priest would give me ten days' penance at confessional.

Salome. *(Flinging out her hands)* Ten days' penance or a life without a husband. Which do you choose?

Tonia. I will tell you. She chooses the husband. What do we do, Salome?

Salome. You run and find this carver of doors. Tell him that a great scandal has happened—that Berta has fallen in the well.

Tonia. *(Whose dramatic imagination has begun to work)* Because she could not live without him—

Berta. You tell him that and I will scratch out both your eyes!

Tonia. On Sunday?

Berta. *(Sullenly)* On any day.

Salome. Tell him that Berta has fallen in the well, and that you think she is dying.

Tonia. Is that all?

Berta. Is that not enough?

Salome. *(Entranced with the idea)* Oh, it will be a great scene, with Berta so pale in her bed, and Fidel kneeling in tears beside it.

Berta. I want you to know that I am a modest girl.

Salome. *(Irritated)* You can lie down on the floor,

15

then. *(Glaring at* Tonia*)* What are you standing there for? Run!

Tonia. *(Starts toward the archway, then comes back)* But—where will I go?

Salome. To the place where all men go with a broken heart—the saloon. Are you going to stand there all day?

(Tonia *gives a little gasp and runs out through the arch.)*

Berta. I do not like this idea. If Fidel finds out it is a trick, he will be angrier than ever.

Salome. But if he does not find out the truth until after you are married—what difference will it make?

Berta. He might beat me.

Salome. Leave that worry until after you are married. *(Inspecting* Berta*)* Now how will we make you look pale? Have you any flour? Corn meal might do.

Berta. No! No! I will not do it.

Salome. Now, Berta, be reasonable.

Berta. If I had really fallen down the well, it would be different. But I did not fall down it.

Salome. Do you not want Fidel to come back to you? Are you in love with him?

Berta. Yes, I do love him. And I will play no tricks on him. If he loves the Celestina better than he does me— *(With great generosity)* he can marry her.

Salome. *(Pleading with such idiocy)* But Tonia has gone down to get him. If he comes back and finds you alive—he will be angrier than ever.

Berta. *(Firmly)* This is your idea. You can get out of it the best way you can. But Fidel will not see me lying down on a bed, nor on a floor, nor any place else.

Salome. Then there is only one thing to do.

Berta. What is that?

Salome. You will go into the house, and I will tell him that you are too sick to see him.

Berta. That will be just as bad as the other.

Salome. How can it be? Then if he finds out it is

16

a trick, he will blame me, and you can pretend you knew nothing of it. I do not care how angry he is. I do not want to marry him.

BERTA. *(With pleased excitement)* Then he could not be angry with me, could he? I mean if he thought I had nothing to do with it? And I would not have to do penance either, would I?

SALOME. Not one day of penance. Tonia should have found him by now. *(Goes to the arch and peers through)* Here they come—and Fidel is running half a block in front of her.

BERTA. *(Joyously)* Then he does love me!

SALOME. Into the house with you. You can watch through the window.

BERTA. *(On stoop)* Now, remember, if he gets angry, this was your idea.

SALOME. *(Claps her hands)* And what a beautiful idea it is!

(BERTA *disappears into the house.* SALOME *looks about her, then dashes over to her own stoop, sits down, flings her shawl over her face, and begins to moan loudly, rocking back and forth. In a moment* FIDEL *dashes through the arch, and stops, out of breath, at seeing* SALOME.)

FIDEL. *(Gasping)* Berta!

SALOME. *(Whose moaning grows louder)* Poor darling, poor darling. She was so young.

FIDEL. *(Desperately)* She is—she is dead?

SALOME. *(Wailing)* She will make such a beautiful corpse. Poor darling. Poor darling.

TONIA. *(Exhausted and out of breath, has reached the arch. Looks about her in astonishment)* Why, where is Berta? Did she go into the house?

SALOME. *(In normal tones)* Of course she went into the house, you fool. Did she not jump down the well? *(Remembering* FIDEL) Poor darling.

TONIA. *(Blankly)* Did she really jump down it? I thought she just fell in by accident.

SALOME. *(Rising, grimly)* Are you telling this story

17

—or am I? *(Wailing)* Now she can never go to the plaza again.

(FIDEL *looks helplessly from* TONIA, *who cannot quite get the details of the story straight, to* SALOME, *who is having a beautiful time mourning.)*

FIDEL. Where is she? I want to see her.

TONIA. *(Coming out of her trance)* She is right in here. Did you say she was on the bed or on the floor, Salome?

SALOME. *(Getting between them and* BERTA'S *door)* You don't want to see her, Fidel. You know how people look after they've been drowned.

TONIA. But he was supposed to see her. That was why you sen—

SALOME. *(Glaring at her)* Tonia, dear, suppose that you let me tell the story. After all, I was here and you were not.

FIDEL. *(Exploding)* For the love of the saints, tell me! Is she dead?

SALOME. *(Thinking this over)* Well—not exactly.

FIDEL. You mean—you mean there is hope?

SALOME. I would say there was great hope.

FIDEL. *(Takes off his hat and mops his face)* What can I do? Oh, if I could only see her—

SALOME. If you would go to the church and light a candle to Our Blessed Lady and ask her to forgive you for getting angry with Berta—perhaps things will arrange themselves.

FIDEL. Do you think she will get well soon?

SALOME. With a speed that will amaze you.

FIDEL. I will go down and light the candle right now.

(As he turns to leave, who should come through the archway but CELESTINA GARCIA. *She can match temper for temper with* BERTA *any day, and right now she is on the warpath. Brushing past these* THREE *as though they did not exist, she goes up to* BERTA'S *door and pounds on it.)*

CELESTINA. I dare you to come out and call this Celestina Garcia a four-nosed shrew to her face.

18

SALOME. *(Trying to push* FIDEL *through the arch)* You had best run to the church.

FIDEL. *(Pushing past her and going up to* CELESTINA) How dare you speak like that to a poor drowned soul?

SALOME. *(To* CELESTINA) Why do you not go away? We never needed you so little.

CELESTINA. So she is pretending to be drowned, eh? Is that her coward's excuse?

BERTA. *(Through window)* Who dares to call Berta Cantu a coward?

CELESTINA. You know well enough who calls you, and I the daughter of Don Nimfo Garcia.

TONIA. Ai, Salome! And now Fidel will know that Berta was not drowned at all.

FIDEL. *(Who has been listening to this conversation with growing surprise and suspicion, now turns furiously toward* BERTA'S *house)* Not drowned, eh? So this was a trick to bring me back, eh? I am through with your tricks, you hear me? Through with them!

BERTA. *(Through window)* You stay right there until I come out. *(She disappears from view.)*

FIDEL. *(Turning to* SALOME) I see your hand in this.

SALOME. The more fool you to be taken in by a woman's tricks.

CELESTINA. What care I for tricks? No woman is going to call me names!

BERTA. *(Coming through the door)* You keep silence, Celestina Garcia. I will deal with you in a minute. And as for you, Fidel Duran—

FIDEL. *(Stormily)* As for me, I am finished with all women. The world will see me no more. I will enter a monastery and carve as many doors as I like. Do you hear me, Berta Cantu?

BERTA. *(Putting both hands over her ears)* What do I care for your quack, quack, quack!

FIDEL. Now she calls me a duck! Good afternoon to you! *(He stalks out with wounded dignity.)*

CELESTINA. *(Catching* BERTA *by the shoulder and*

19

swinging her around) I ask you again: Did you call me a four-nosed shrew?

BERTA. I did, and I will repeat it with the greatest of pleasure. You are a four-nosed shrew and a three-eyed frog!

CELESTINA. I have always looked on you as my friend—you pink-toed cat!

BERTA. And I have always trusted you—you sly robber of bridegrooms! *(She raises her hand to slap* CELESTINA. SALOME *catches it.)*

SALOME. This is Sunday, Berta! And Sunday costs five pesos.

TONIA. If you had to pay a fine for starting a fight on top of losing Fidel— Ay, that would be terrible.

*(*BERTA *and* CELESTINA *glare at each other, and then slowly begin to circle each other, spitting out their insults as they do so.)*

CELESTINA. It is my honor that is making me fight, or I would wait until tomorrow.

BERTA. If I had five pesos to throw away, I would pull out your dangling tongue—leaving only the flapping roots.

CELESTINA. Ha! I make a nose at your words.

BERTA. As for you—you eater of ugly smelling cheese—

(They jump at each other, but remember the penalty just in time and pull back. Again they begin to circle around, contenting themselves with making faces at each other. SALOME *suddenly clasps her hands.)*

SALOME. You are both certain that you want to fight today?

CELESTINA. Why else do you think I came here?

BERTA. These insults have gone too far to stop now.

SALOME. The only thing that stands in the way is the five pesos for the Sunday fine.

TONIA. And five pesos is a lot of money.

SALOME. Then the only thing to do is to play the fingers.

CELESTINA. What?

BERTA. Eh?

SALOME. Precisely. Whoever loses strikes the first blow and pays the fine. Then you can fight as much as you like.

TONIA. *(With awed admiration)* Ay, Salome, you have so many brains.

CELESTINA. *(Doubtfully)* It is a big risk.

BERTA. *(Shrugging)* Perhaps you are afraid of taking a risk.

CELESTINA. I am not afraid of anything. But Tonia will have to be the judge. Salome is too clever.

BERTA. Very well. But Salome has to stand behind you to see that you do not cheat. I would not trust you any more than I would a mouse near a piece of fresh bacon.

CELESTINA. *(Pulls back her clenched fist, then thinks better of it, and speaks with poor grace)* Very well.

(CELESTINA *and* BERTA *stand facing each other.* TONIA *stands between them up on the stoop.* SALOME *stands behind* CELESTINA.)

TONIA. *(Feeling a little nervous over this great honor of judging)* Both arms behind your backs. *(The* GIRLS *link their arms behind them)* Now, when I drop my hand, Berta will guess first as Celestina brings her fingers forward. The first girl to guess correctly twice wins. Are you ready? (ALL *nod)* I am going to drop my arm.

SALOME. Celestina, put out your fingers before Berta guesses. We will have no cheating.

CELESTINA. *(Sullenly)* Very well.

(She puts out two fingers behind her, and SALOME, *seeing this, raises up her arm with two fingers extended, opening and closing them scissors fashion.* BERTA *frowns a little as she looks up at the signal and* CELESTINA, *seeing this, swings around and*

looks at SALOME, *who promptly grins warmly and pretends to be waving at* BERTA. CELESTINA *then looks at* TONIA.)

BERTA. Very well.
CELESTINA. *(Guessing as* BERTA *swings her arm forward)* Three.

(BERTA *triumphantly holds up one finger. Biting her lip,* CELESTINA *starts to swing forward her own arm.* SALOME, *intent on signalling* BERTA, *holds up her own five fingers spread wide, and does not notice until too late that* CELESTINA *has swung around to watch her.)*

CELESTINA. *(Screaming)* So I cheat, eh?

(With that she gives SALOME *a resounding slap on the cheek. The next moment the* TWO WOMEN *are mixed up in a beautiful howling, grunting fight, while* TONIA *and* BERTA, *wide-eyed, cling together and give the* TWO WOMEN *as much space as possible. Let it be understood that this is only a fight of kicking, hair-pulling and scratching. There is no man involved, nor a point of honor. Rather a matter of angry pride. So the* TWO *are not attempting to mutilate each other. They are simply gaining satisfaction. The grand finale comes when* CELESTINA *knocks* SALOME *to the ground and sits on her.)*

CELESTINA. *(Breathing hard)* There! That was worth five pesos.
TONIA. You have to pay it. And Don Nimfo will be angry with you.
CELESTINA. *(Pulling herself to her feet)* I am too tired to fight any more now, but I will be back next Tuesday, Berta, and then I will beat you up.
BERTA. *(Sniffing)* If you can.
CELESTINA. *(Warningly)* And there is no fine on Tuesday.

22

BERTA. Come any day you like. I will be ready for you.

TONIA. *(To* CELESTINA*)* You should be ashamed to fight.

CELESTINA. Who are you to talk to me? *(Stamps her foot at* TONIA*, who jumps behind* BERTA*)* Good afternoon, my brave little rabbits!

(She staggers out as straight as she can, but as she reaches the archway she feels a twinge of agony and is forced to limp. By this time SALOME *has gathered together what strength she has left, and she slowly stands up. Once erect, she looks at* BERTA *and* TONIA *as though she were considering boiling in oil too good for them.)*

SALOME. *(With repressed fury)* My friends. My very good friends.

TONIA. *(Frightened)* Now, Salome—

SALOME. *(Screaming)* Do not speak to me! Either of you! *(She manages to get to the door of her house)* When I need help, do you give me aid? No! But just you wait—both of you!

TONIA. What are you going to do?

SALOME. I am going to wait for a week-day, and then I am going to beat up both of you at once. One *(She takes a deep breath)* with each hand! *(She nearly falls through the door of her house.)*

BERTA. *(With false bravado)* Who is afraid of her?

TONIA. I am. Salome is very strong. It is all your fault. If you had not gotten mad at Fidel, this would not have happened.

BERTA. *(Snapping at her)* You leave Fidel out of this.

TONIA. *(Beginning to cry)* When Salome beats me up, that will be your fault too.

BERTA. Stop crying!

TONIA. I am not a good fighter, but I can tell Fidel the truth about how you would not jump down the well to win him back.

BERTA. You open your mouth to Fidel and I will push you in the well.

Tonia. You will not have strength enough to push a baby in the well when they get through with you.

Berta. Get out! Get out of here!

(She stamps her foot at Tonia *and the girl, frightened, gives a squeak and runs into her own house.* Berta *looks after her, then, beginning to sniffle, she goes over and sits on the well. She acts like a child who has been told that it is not proper for little girls to cry, and she is very much in need of a handkerchief. Just then* Fidel *sticks his head around the arch.)*

Fidel. *(Once more the plaintive goat)* Berta. (Berta *half jumps, then pretends not to hear him.* Fidel *enters cautiously, not taking his eyes off of* Berta's *stiff back. He moves around at the back, skirts* Tonia's *house, then works his way round to her)* Berta.

Berta. *(Sniffling)* What is it?

Fidel. *(Circling the back of the well)* Are you crying, Berta?

Berta. *(Stubbornly)* No!

Fidel. *(Sitting beside her)* Yes, you are. I can see you crying.

Berta. If you can see, why do you ask, then?

Fidel. I am sorry we quarrelled, Berta.

Berta. Are you?

Fidel. Are you sorry?

Berta. No!

Fidel. I was hoping you were, because—do you know whom I saw on the plaza?

Berta. Grandfather Devil.

Fidel. Don Nimfo himself.

Berta. Perhaps you saw the Celestina, too.

Fidel. *(Placatingly)* Now, Berta, you know I do not care if I never see the Celestina again. *(Pulls out a handkerchief and extends it to her)* Here, wipe your face with this.

Berta. I have a handkerchief of my own. *(Nevertheless she takes it, and wipes her eyes and then blows her nose.)*

24

FIDEL. Don Nimfo said I could carve the church doors for him. But he said I would have to move to Topo Grande to work on them. He said I had to leave right away.

BERTA. *(Perking up her interest)* You mean—move away from here?

FIDEL. And I was wondering if we could get married tomorrow. I know this is very sudden, Berta, but after all, think how long I have waited to carve a church door.

BERTA. Tomorrow. *(She looks toward SALOME'S house)* They would both be too sore to do anything by tomorrow.

FIDEL. *(Too concerned with his own plans to hear what she is saying)* Of course I know that you may not be able to forgive me—

BERTA. Fidel, I want you to understand that if I do marry you tomorrow—that means we will leave here tomorrow, eh?

FIDEL. Ay, yes. I have to be in Topo Grande on Tuesday.

BERTA. I hope you will always understand what a great thing I have done for you. It is not every girl who would forgive so easily as I.

FIDEL. *(Humbly)* Indeed, I know that, Berta.

BERTA. Are you quite sure that we will leave here tomorrow?

FIDEL. Quite sure.

BERTA. Very well. I will marry you.

FIDEL. *(Joyfully)* Berta! *(Bends forward to kiss her. She jumps up.)*

BERTA. Just a moment. We are not married yet. Do you think that I am just any girl that you can kiss me —like that! *(She snaps her fingers.)*

FIDEL. *(Humbly)* I thought—just this once—

BERTA. *(Gravely thoughtful)* Well, perhaps—just this once—you may kiss my hand.

(As he kisses it

THE CURTAINS CLOSE

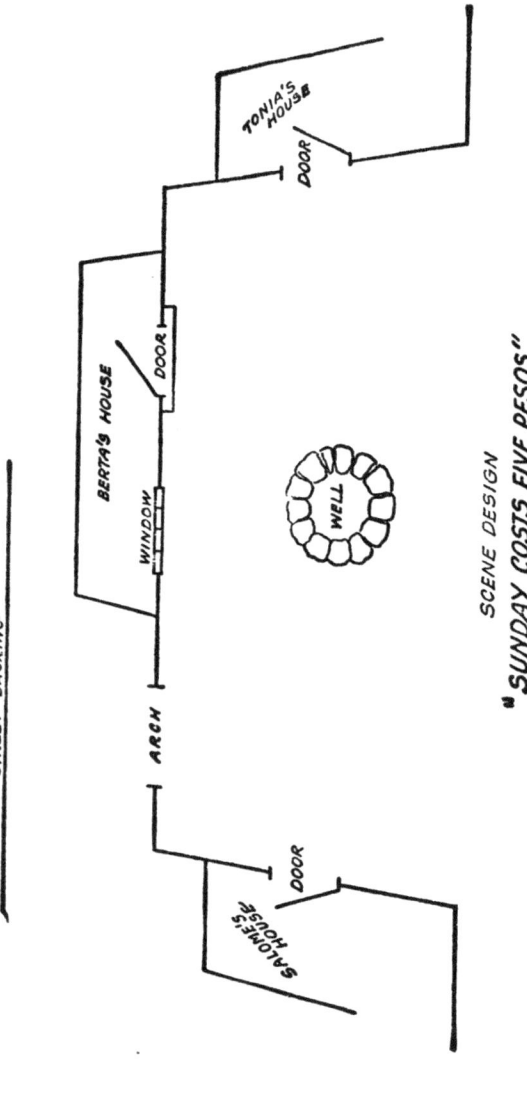

STREET BACKING

TONIA'S HOUSE

DOOR

BERTA'S HOUSE

DOOR

WINDOW

WELL

ARCH

DOOR

SAMUEL'S HOUSE

SCENE DESIGN

"SUNDAY COSTS FIVE PESOS"

SUNDAY COSTS FIVE PESOS

STORY OF THE PLAY

Sunday Costs Five Pesos is a hilarious comedy of small town Mexican folk. The author tells us it is based on an old Mexican law that is still enforced in many of the small villages of the Republic. No one knows the reason for its existence, but its phrasing goes straight to the point: "A woman who starts a fight on Sunday must pay a fine of five pesos." Since Sunday alone is stressed, the result is that what fighting is done is generally held over for week days. Berta suspects her lover, Fidel, of flirting with Celestina. Fidel tries to explain but she sends him away grieving. She soon begins to weaken, however, and is overcome with regret. Her friends, Salome and Tonia, concoct a story that Berta has fallen in the well and Tonia hurries after Fidel to break the news to him. He comes flying back to the scene and they insinuate that Berta is in very bad condition indeed. They send Fidel off to burn a candle in the church to atone for his getting angry with his sweetheart. Celestina appears on the scene, anxious to have it out with Berta for calling her names. It being Sunday, they are hesitant about fighting on account of the fine, so they engage in a guessing contest. Celestina catches Salome cheating and the contest winds up with her sitting on top of Salome after a fierce fight. When Berta is alone Fidel comes back and a reconciliation is brought about and marriage is in sight.

OTHER TITLES AVAILABLE FROM SAMUEL FRENCH

SOLDADERA
Josephina Niggli

Drama / 1m, 7f

A very affecting account of feminine heroism. It is taut with suspense and doubt, and gives some supreme characterizations of women acting under stress during the terrible Mexican Revolution. Bold and gripping.

OTHER TITLES AVAILABLE FROM SAMUEL FRENCH

LANDSCAPE WITH WAITRESS
Robert Pine

Comedy / 1m, 1f / Interior

Arthur Granger, an unsuccessful novelist who lives a Walter Mitty like fantasy existence, is dining in an Italian restaurant with only one waitress and one customer–himself. As he selects his dinner, he fantasizes about a romantic conquest involving far fetched plots. The waitress portrays characters in his fantasy. Soon, Arthur is chattering at such a clip that his sanity is in doubt. He finishes his dinner and goes home, ending as he began– as a lover manque.

"A devious and slightly demented comedy."
– New York Times